WALT DISNEY
PICTURES PRESENTS

DINOSAUR

Zını's Big Adventure

Adapted from the film by Dona Smith

DISNEY
PRESS

NEW YORK

Printed in the United States of America.

First Edition

1 3 5 7 9 10 8 6 4 2

This book is set in 16-point Berkeley Book.

Library of Congress Catalog Card Number: 99-68941

ISBN: 0-7868-4408-6

For more Disney Press fun, visit www.disneybooks.com

Chapter One

Sixty million years ago a herd of dinosaurs lived in paradise. Then one day . . .

CRASH! A carnotaur smashed through the trees. As the herd of dinosaurs fled in terror, it stomped on a nest, destroying all the eggs but one.

The egg tumbled down a cliff into a river. A pteranodon snatched it from the water. It carried the egg across the ocean to a faraway land.

Okay, so I didn't exactly see the whole thing. So what? But I figure that's pretty close to what happened. How else could a dinosaur egg end up so far from home?

My name is Zini. I was the first one on Lemur Island to see the egg. Well, maybe not *exactly* the first, but almost. My lemur friends Yar and Plio and I spotted it at the same time.

The egg hatched right in front of our eyes.

I had a feeling something important had just happened. I was right. One day the little guy would help me save a whole dinosaur nation.

The adventure that made me a hero began a few years later, when I was a teenager. The scaly

little baby had grown into a huge dinosaur. I named him Aladar, and I taught him everything I knew.

Anyway, it was supposed to be my big night—it was the courtship ritual, at the Ritual Tree, where I would win over the prettiest, furriest female lemur around.

Things didn't quite work out the way I'd planned.

I leaped for a branch, missed, and landed in a bush. After that, nobody paid any attention to me. I figured I'd just go ahead and hang by myself.

Suddenly a bright streak of light sliced through the sky. Then there was another, and another. Soon the sky was full of fireworks.

As I watched in amazement . . . *WHOOSH!* A huge fireball exploded

5

in the sky. Then it was dark and quiet again.

Through the silence there came an eerie sound—*WHOOOOOOO!*

BOOM! The earth rumbled. The whole world rocked like crazy, as if it was going to rip apart at the seams.

The sky hurled bombs of flame. The trees caught fire, and blazing branches came crashing down.

Yar, Plio, Suri, and I climbed aboard Aladar. The blazing wave of flame chased us over the cliff, and we swam across the ocean to dry land.

Aladar staggered onto a deserted beach. The sand was covered with cinders. The air was full of ash and smoke.

Aladar collapsed, gasping for breath. We

slid off his back, coughing and choking. We could see Lemur Island across the water, completely destroyed.

We were the only ones left.

Chapter Two

Aladar had been walking for hours. There was nothing but rocks and dust as far as we could see.

Out of the corner of my eye, I saw something moving up ahead. I tapped Aladar on the shoulder.

"Look!"

Aladar took off after it until he came to the edge of a ridge. Aladar moved slowly down into the gully below. We looked all around, but didn't find a thing.

Then we heard something.

CLICK . . . CLICK . . . CLICK.

We looked up and saw a strange creature sitting on a rocky ledge. There was another beside it. They were everywhere!

Suddenly, one of the creatures bared a row of sharp teeth and hissed. *SSSSSSSS!!!!!!* It definitely wasn't a friendly greeting.

Aladar jumped back. I didn't know it then, but these creatures were raptors, savage and deadly.

They suddenly began lunging at Aladar, attacking from all sides!

But then the strangest thing happened.

The raptors began to fall back as the ground rumbled and shook.

A big creature blasted through the dust. It was a dinosaur—another Aladar. But this dinosaur was bigger—and uglier!

WHAM! He knocked Aladar off his feet. "STAY OUT OF MY WAY!" he roared. Wow! He was ugly *and* mean.

As Aladar scrambled up again another beast pushed past.

"You heard Kron! Move it!"

I rubbed my eyes and peered through the swirling dust. There were dinosaurs in

front of us, behind us, beside us. They were big . . . and *bigger*. There were hundreds of them!

WHACK! Aladar got slammed again. He did a double take. This dinosaur was *pretty*.

"OW! Watch it!" She eyeballed Aladar and snorted with disgust as she went by.

The dinosaurs surged onward, down the bluff toward a rocky mesa. Soon they had left us behind—but not alone.

The choice seemed simple enough to me. Either we go with the big guys or get eaten by the raptors.

CLICK! CLICK! CLICK! CLICK! The raptors were closing in. I let Aladar make the call.

"Hang on!" he cried. He took off after the dinosaurs.

Chapter Three

The sun was going down when the Herd finally stopped. "We'll rest here for the night," Kron bellowed to his second in command, a big iguanodon named Bruton.

Bruton relayed the orders. Everyone surged forward at once.

"All this pushing and shoving just to find a place to sleep," cried a big dinosaur. "I'm not used to such behavior."

She was the biggest creature I had ever seen.

"Come on, Baylene!" snorted a smaller dinosaur. "Ya wanna get to the Nesting Grounds alive, show some backbone."

Aladar ambled over. "Hey, there. My name's Aladar."

"This is Eema, a styracosaur," Baylene said, gesturing to the smaller dino by her side. "My name is Baylene. I'm a brachiosaur." She

squinted at Yar. "Oh, dear. What an unfortunate blemish."

"Excuse me?" Yar sputtered indignantly.

"We heard you say something about the Nesting Grounds," Plio said in a friendly voice.

Eema smiled. "It is the most beautiful place there is, child." She sighed. "It's where the Herd goes to have their babies. But that Fireball put us back a spell, and the eggs might come before we get there."

"And we're being driven unmercifully," Baylene said sadly.

"By who?" Aladar asked.

"Kron, the Herd's head honcho," Eema answered wearily.

As if he knew we were talking about him, Kron suddenly appeared. He came swaggering through the dust with Bruton and the pretty girl dinosaur beside him.

"Hey! Uh . . . excuse me . . . Kron? Got a second?" Aladar asked bravely.

"Who are you?" Kron asked.

"Uh . . . Aladar. I was back here talking to these guys." He nodded toward Eema and Baylene. "They're having a hard time keeping up . . . so, you know, maybe you could slow it down a bit?"

"Hmmm . . . let the weak set the pace." Kron gave a snort. "Better let me do the thinking from now on, Aladar." He and Bruton stomped away, but Neera lagged behind.

"Don't worry." She smiled at Aladar.

"That's how my brother treats newcomers, no matter how charming they are."

"You sure know how to catch a girl's eye, stud!" I said, teasing Aladar.

"I wouldn't be catching nobody's eye, if I was you," said Eema. "'Specially Neera's! You just mind what Kron tells you."

"Better to keep our heads down with this bunch than get 'em bitten off by those things," Aladar said.

Raptors. They were still following us, watching and waiting for their chance to attack.

Chapter Four

It felt as if I had barely closed my eyes when I heard a commotion. Dinosaurs were milling around. I leaped on Aladar's head.

"Hey, Aladar! Hellooo? Anybody in there?" I tapped his scaly head.

"What's the hurry?" Aladar said sleepily.

"Something's up."

"Rise and shine!" Bruton announced.

"The charm never stops around here," I mumbled.

Bruton whirled around. "You say something?"

"Uh, no, no, sir." Aladar mumbled, covering for me.

"Unless you got a death wish, you and that little parasite better get moving." Parasite? Like *he* could talk, the big ugly reptile.

Then I caught sight of Neera up ahead. "Hey, hey, hey! There's your girlfriend!"

"What are you talking about?" Aladar asked.

"You know . . . Neera, scaly skin, yellow eyes, big ankles. Let me give you a little help from 'The Love Monkey.'" Before Aladar could stop me, I climbed on top of his head.

"Oh, baby!" I whistled, then I ducked out of sight.

Neera turned around and gave Aladar a dirty look. "Jerk-a-saurus."

Whoops! But right then Aladar had other things to worry about. Bruton was bellowing Kron's orders.

"Listen up! There is no water till we reach the other side. And you better keep up. If a

predator catches you, you're on your own!"

On and on we went, across packed and dusty earth, over sand and hills and rocks. Finally, we came to the foot of another hill.

"The lake!" Eema sighed.

Everyone started rushing up the hill. We struggled to keep up.

"Come on, Eema!" Aladar urged. "Remember 'water'? The wet stuff?"

Eema brightened a little. "Well, it's time to refresh my memory. I'm going to walk right into that lake until the water's up to my eye-balls and soak it all in."

We were the last to reach the top of the hill. I was expecting to see everyone jumping around and laughing. Instead the Herd was quiet.

I squinted and looked up ahead. Where was this big lake I'd heard so much about?

It had dried up.

What were we going to do now?

Chapter Five

Kron sent Bruton up ahead with a scout to look for water.

"You have to be strong," he announced to the Herd. "Keep moving!"

I looked around at the exhausted, dusty bunch. *Keep moving?* They were barely *breathing.*

Neera hurried over to her brother.

"Kron, we've never gone so long without water. If we keep going like this we'll lose half the Herd."

"Then we'll save the half that deserves to live," Kron said, and walked away.

Neera stared after him.

Eema suddenly trotted down into the dry lake bed and started rolling around in the sand as if water were still there.

"There was always water here before," she gasped. "Nice water and plenty of mud."

Aladar tried to get her on her feet. "You gotta get up," he said desperately.

Baylene began walking toward them.

SQUISH. SQUISH.

"Baylene. Don't move," Aladar said.

"What's wrong?" Baylene took another step.

SQUISH.

"Do ya hear that?" I pointed to the water that was pooling around Baylene's big feet.

"I sure do!" Aladar started digging. I helped. Soon there was a big hole filled with water.

Plio, Suri, and Yar helped Eema struggle to her feet.

"That's it, Eema," Baylene said. "Come and drink."

"Water! C'mon!" Aladar called to the Herd.

"He found water!" Neera trumpeted.

Kron marched right up to us.

"Kron, look . . . all we had to do was dig and—" Aladar began.

"Good. Now, get out of the way." He stuck his face in the water and began to gulp.

That was all the Herd needed to see. They began a mad stampede down the hill.

"Wait! Wait!" Aladar protested. "There's enough for everyone."

Nobody paid any attention to him. Dinosaurs plowed into one another as they tried to get to the water. Old Eema was nearly trampled.

"That's it, keep pushing and shoving. That's very helpful," Aladar grumbled. He began guiding Eema through the sea of bodies.

I spotted Neera watching Aladar shield Eema. She was used to her brother Kron's ways, and Aladar just kept surprising her every minute.

Chapter Six

Kron decided to make camp at the lake bed.

"Here, now. You just take a foot and *press*." Aladar was playing big brother and showing a dinosaur kid how to get water.

Out of the corner of my eye, I saw Neera wander over.

"I see you like kids," she said.

"Well, the skinny ones can be kind of

chewy." They both laughed. Hmmm . . . old Aladar was actually making conversation. I scooted closer to eavesdrop.

"I'm Aladar. The jerk-a-saurus."

"Sorry about that." Neera scuffed her foot in the dirt. "Why *did* you help that old one?" Neera asked.

"What else could we do? Leave them behind?"

"It happens all the time," Neera said. "You don't survive if you're not . . ."

"Strong enough," Aladar finished for her. "Is that you talking? Or your brother?"

Neera thought for a moment. "I don't know."

"Everyone counts . . . strong . . . weak . . . doesn't matter."

"I bet you want some water." Aladar started to dig.

"Can I try?" Neera asked.

"Sure. Just press."

Neera pushed her foot into the dirt. She smiled as she saw the water appear.

They both bent to drink at the same time.

"Oops." Aladar was embarrassed. The two of them stood there, staring at each other. I was starting to feel kinda mushy myself.

But then suddenly, "RRROOOOAARRR!" The bloodcurdling sound cut through the night.

I saw Neera and Aladar rush over to Kron. "What's going on?" Neera asked.

"Carnotaurs!" he answered. "If we don't

keep moving, they will catch up to us."

"You can't do that!" Aladar objected. "The ones in the back will never make it." Kron ignored him.

Aladar hurried after Kron. "You can't sacrifice them like that!" he cried.

"Hold it!" Aladar called to the gathering Herd. "That could be you back there . . . or you."

Kron lunged, knocking Aladar to the ground. A menacing growl erupted from his throat.

"If you ever interfere again, I'll kill you." He glared at Neera. "Stay away from him!"

Aladar jumped to his feet and started toward Kron.

"Aladar, no!" Neera cried. "You just . . . just go! I'll be okay."

Aladar didn't want to leave Neera. But he couldn't leave Eema, Baylene, and the rest of us to fend for ourselves, either.

"Let's go!" Aladar called. "Carnotaurs!"

"Carno *what*?" Yar jumped on his back.

"A mouth full of teeth with a bad attitude," Eema said.

Aladar took off at a run. "Come on, you guys! We're gonna get left behind!"

"Aladar, slow down!" Plio cried.

Aladar looked up ahead. Neera and the rest of the Herd were disappearing into the distance. With a desperate sigh, he turned and came back to us.

Chapter Seven

Our scraggly group had camped out for the night in a cave to escape the storm that came up.

We had stumbled across Bruton, who had been so badly wounded by a carnotaur that he couldn't keep up with the Herd. He had reluctantly followed us into the cave to get out of the storm, but kept to himself off in the corner.

I watched as Plio slowly crept to his side. Bruton eyed her suspiciously.

A small spiky plant grew between the rocks. She broke it open. Thick, gooey liquid oozed out.

"This plant grew on our island. It will make you feel better," she explained as she patted the goo on his wounds.

After a moment Bruton nodded toward Aladar. "Why doesn't he let them accept their fate? I've accepted mine."

"And what is your fate?" Plio asked.

"To die here. It's the way things are."

Plio took a deep breath. "Only if you give up, Bruton. It's your choice, not your fate."

Plio had given him something to think about. He watched as we huddled together to stay warm, but he didn't join us.

CRASH! A clap of thunder woke me and I jumped up.

"Sssshhh! Carnotaurs!" Bruton whispered. He crouched next to Aladar.

I saw two huge silhouettes on the wall. They were shadows of the beasts that stood just outside the cave.

We began creeping deeper into the cave.

My heart was thudding so loud I was sure the carnotaurs could hear it. Baylene was shaking so much her head brushed against a rock.

PLUNK!

Baylene gasped as the stone rolled toward the cave entrance.

One of the carnotaurs sniffed it. They both peered into the darkness.

FLAAASHHH! Another bolt of lightning struck. The carnotaurs saw us!

CHARGE! They thundered into the cave.

CHOMP! One of the creatures bit down on Aladar's tail. It began dragging him backward.

KABLAM! Bruton slammed the surprised carnotaurs aside and freed Aladar.

"I'll hold them off. Save the others!" Bruton yelled to Aladar.

Bruton stood his ground as the two carnotaurs pounced. Aladar ran toward us.

Bruton was fighting bravely, but he was no match for the carnotaurs. Then he made a choice that would save our lives.

He rammed a pillar with every last bit of strength he had.

CRACK! The roof began to collapse.

"Bruton . . . no!" Aladar roared.

The cave tumbled down on Bruton and the carnotaurs. In seconds they were buried under an avalanche of boulders!

Aladar began clawing through the rocks.

"Bruton!" he shouted.

Aladar kept digging. He found Bruton, but he had died saving us from the carnotaurs.

"You did what you could," Plio said sadly. Suddenly, the rocks started moving—could one of the carnotaurs still be alive? We didn't stick around to find out.

Chapter Eight

There was nowhere to go but deeper into the pitch-black cave.

Suddenly, I saw that a wall of boulders blocked our path.

"What do we do now?" Yar asked.

"I guess we go back," Aladar said wearily.

My heart sank. If we went back we might

run into the carnotaur. I was beginning to think we were doomed. Then suddenly, I got a whiff of fresh air!

"Hold on a minute. Do you smell that?"

"Yeah!" Suri sniffed.

We both scampered ahead. I climbed up on a ledge and started to dig the rocks away.

A shaft of light shot into the cave.

"Everybody stand back. We're outta here!" Aladar yelled. He got a running start and smashed into the wall of rocks.

The rocks began to move. The shaft of light grew wider. Then more stones began tumbling down.

Aladar leaped out of the way as the wall suddenly collapsed. The light disappeared.

"Noooo!" Aladar beat against the rocks with his feet.

After a few minutes he slumped to the ground in defeat. "We're not meant to survive."

"Oh, yes we are!" Baylene piped up. She strutted over to Aladar.

"We're here, aren't we? How dare you give

up? Shame on you, shame on you, shame on you."

She rammed into the wall. The rest of us joined in to help Baylene push—everyone but Aladar.

We groaned and strained, but our legs kept slipping in the dirt.

Our courage got Aladar fired up again. He stood shoulder to shoulder with us, pushing with all his might. As we all pushed *together* . . .

CRRAAACK!

There was a thunderous rumble. The stones gave way, and bright sunlight flooded the cave. We stepped through the wall of dust and onto a ledge. We couldn't believe our eyes!

A beautiful landscape spread before us. There were endless fields of green grass, blue sky, and trees. An enormous, crystal-clear lake sparkled in the sun. It was paradise!

"The Nesting Grounds," Eema breathed.

"Our new home." Plio hugged Suri.

"Not bad!" said Aladar. "But where's the Herd?"

"Oh, they'll get here soon enough . . ." Eema's voice trailed off as she turned around. "I spoke too soon."

She pointed up ahead. A mountain of rocks and boulders were piled in front of a nearby canyon.

"That is the way we used to get in here."

Aladar gasped. "They'll never make it over that!" He turned to leave.

"Kron will eat you alive!" Eema yelled.

But Aladar was already on his way back through the cave. Although I wasn't there to witness what happened next, I've spread the word of Aladar's bravery and made it legend. He can thank me for that!

He sped over the land in search of the Herd.

Finally he spotted the Herd up ahead. Kron was trying to lead them into the valley by the usual route, but the path was blocked.

"Don't give up!" Kron bellowed. "Our survival, our future, is over these rocks!"

Exhausted, the Herd started up the dangerous slope. But the rocks were loose, and the dinosaurs kept losing their footing.

"Kron! A carnotaur is coming!" Aladar yelled.

"Keep moving!" Kron ordered.

"Stop!" Aladar insisted. "I've been to the valley. There is a safer way! We gotta go now!"

Kron glared at him. "Go where?"

"We can't get over these rocks. There's a sheer drop on the other side."

"Kron, listen to him," Neera urged.

With a mighty lunge, Kron knocked Aladar to the ground. Aladar leaped up, and lashed out at Kron.

Enraged, Kron pulled himself up, ready to attack again.

KABLAM! A dinosaur broadsided him. It was Neera!

She helped Aladar to his feet. Together they headed out of the canyon. As Kron stared in

amazement, the Herd began to follow.

"RRROOAAAR!" A carnotaur!

The Herd was so scared they began to follow Kron up the rocky mountain.

"No!" Aladar thundered. "If we scatter, he'll pick us off! Stand together!"

The carnotaur charged toward the Herd.

Instead of running, Aladar stood his ground. Neera stepped beside him. The rest of the dinosaurs followed.

The carnotaur was confused. He didn't know what to do.

The whole Herd closed ranks. They surged toward the carnotaur, bellowing in unison.

The carnotaur spotted Kron, struggling up on the rocks. A lone dinosaur was easy prey.

The carnotaur leaped up the rocky hillside to Kron and hurled him against a wall.

Kron landed on the rocks and didn't move.

SLAM! SLAM! SLAM! Neera charged and rammed the carnotaur.

BLAM! The carnotaur struck back. He hit Neera full force.

KABLAM! Aladar smashed the beast with a
vicious tail swipe.

THWACK! The carnotaur struck back.

Suddenly the rocks under their feet began
to roll. The carnotaur flailed helplessly as the
edge of the cliff crumbled away and he
plunged over the side!

Aladar pulled himself to safety and Neera
ran to his side. The Herd began to cheer.

Aladar led the Herd out of the canyon.

They followed him around the rockslide, into the cave, and back through the tunnels. At last, they reached their beautiful valley—the Nesting Grounds. Aladar turned to them and smiled.

"Welcome home."

I guess you could say we
ever after." Aladar and Ne
course, and started their ow
Aladars. Eema, Baylene, and
being adoring grandparents
And I made some new frien
lady friends, if you get my dri

Well, that's the story of

Walt Disney
PICTURES PRESEN
DIN
tOys

You've found the
last dinosaur egg!
It's Aladar from
Disney's *Dinosaur*.

Dino Alive™! Aladar
You can hatch, "feed," and train your prehistoric pet again and
again! Aladar will walk, talk, and ROAR just like in the movie!

Dino Clash Card Game
It's a prehistoric game of "War." Each player
flips over a card...the most powerful card in
each round wins!

Di
All
co
ey

Look for these and the other Di
Fossil Finder Activity Set & Adve

© Disney

They followed him around the rockslide, into the cave, and back through the tunnels. At last, they reached their beautiful valley—the Nesting Grounds. Aladar turned to them and smiled.

"Welcome home."

Chapter Nine

I guess you could say we all lived "happily ever after." Aladar and Neera fell in love, of course, and started their own family of little Aladars. Eema, Baylene, and Yar got to play at being adoring grandparents to the babies. And I made some new friends . . . some new *lady* friends, if you get my drift!

Well, that's the story of how I helped

ladar save an entire dinosaur nation. I
:ways told him, if we stick together, we can
do *anything*!

What? You think Aladar did it all? Don't be
silly! He couldn't have done it without me.
After all, I'm the one who taught him everything he knows.